Little Red Riding Hood

Story by:
Wilhelm and Jacob Grimm

Adapted by:
Margaret Ann Hughes

Illustrated by:

Russell Hicks Lorann Downer
Theresa Mazurek Rivka
Douglas McCarthy Fay Whitemountain
Allyn Conley-Gorniak Suzanne Lewis
Julie Ann Armstrong

This Book Belongs To:

Jennifer and Victoria Whiston

Use this symbol to match book and cassette.

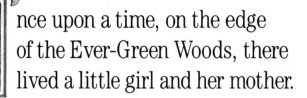

nce upon a time, on the edge of the Ever-Green Woods, there lived a little girl and her mother.

Not too far away, in the middle of the Ever-Green Woods, lived the little girl's grandmother.

Now the grandmother loved her granddaughter very much, so she made her a very pretty red cape with a hood. It was the little girl's favorite thing in the whole world to wear. And because she wore it all the time, she was called Little Red Riding Hood.

One day Little Red Riding Hood received a letter
from her grandmother saying that she was sick
in bed and hoped that her granddaughter
would visit her.

Little Red Riding Hood was very thoughtful.
She quickly baked some nice blueberry muffins,
and then put them in a basket with some peach
preserves, and jelly tarts, and herb tea.

Little Red Riding Hood put on her red cape with
the hood, picked up the basket of goodies, and in
the morning sun, skipped down the path
to her grandmother's house in the woods.

Now deep within the Ever-Green Woods there also
lived a mean and sneaky wolf named Warren.

He was always looking for some kind of trouble to
get himself into. And he most certainly wasn't
someone you could trust.

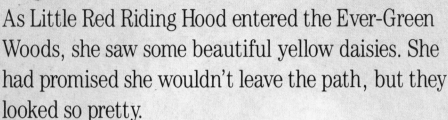

As Little Red Riding Hood entered the Ever-Green Woods, she saw some beautiful yellow daisies. She had promised she wouldn't leave the path, but they looked so pretty.

Little Red Riding Hood left the path and went to pick the flowers. While she wasn't looking, who should appear from behind a tree…but Warren the Wolf!

He frightened Little Red Riding Hood! Oh, he was so sneaky!

Warren then asked what Little Red Riding Hood was doing in the Ever-Green Woods. She told him she was on her way to see her grandmother, who was sick in bed.

Little Red Riding Hood told the wolf about the blueberry muffins, and the peach preserves, and the jelly tarts, and the herb tea.

He smacked his chops as he thought about the food…but I think he was dreaming about an even bigger lunch.

Without even thinking, Little Red Riding Hood told that old wolf exactly how to get to her grandmother's house.

Little Red Riding Hood waved goodbye to Warren, then she continued to pick the flowers. Warren slipped away into the woods. He knew exactly where he was going…to Grandmother's house!

Finally, Little Red Riding Hood had picked a beautiful bouquet of daisies. She took up the basket and went back to the path. She skipped along, going deeper and deeper into the Ever-Green Woods.

Meanwhile, Warren the Wolf reached the grandmother's house in no time at all…long before Little Red Riding Hood.

Warren knocked on the door.

The wolf disguised his voice, so the little old grandmother would think he was her granddaughter. She asked him to come in.

Warren slowly opened the door and very carefully went inside the house. The little old woman was tucked neatly in her bed. She wore her night-gown and a ruffled nightcap on her head.

The wolf slowly crept up to the bed, and with a growl, he showed his teeth!

Just then, Little Red Riding Hood knocked on the door. She arrived just in time!

The wolf grabbed the grandmother and wrapped her in a blanket so she couldn't speak.

Then he put her in the closet, turned the key, and locked her inside. Oh, he was an awful wolf!

Warren raced to the dresser to find a disguise for himself. He started rummaging through the grandmother's clothes.

He found a blue nightgown with a matching nightcap and quickly put them on.

Then with one leap…he jumped into the grand-mother's bed and called to Little Red Riding Hood.

And with his grandmotherly voice, Warren invited her to come in. Little Red Riding Hood lifted the latch…oh, dear…and went inside the house.

Little Red Riding Hood went to her grandmother's bedside and looked at the figure under the blankets with concern.

Warren held the blankets close under his chin. The cap sat low on his head around his face. One couldn't tell he was a wolf in grandmother's clothing!

As Warren looked into the basket of goodies, his eyes got larger and larger! He was a very hungry wolf!

As the wolf nibbled at the food in the basket, the cap on his head began to slip, and one of his ears popped out from under it. Oh, what big ears he had!

The wolf finished the jelly tarts and was about to begin on the muffins. He was still hungry.

Then Warren looked at Little Red Riding Hood with a big, toothy smile. He had enormous, sharp, long white teeth. He certainly wasn't smiling in a friendly way! And he really didn't want muffins to eat!

Warren jumped out of the bed and chased Little Red Riding Hood around and around the room.

As the wolf chased, Little Red Riding Hood screamed, and as Little Red Riding Hood screamed, the grandmother pounded on the closet door.

Oh, my! The wolf caught up to Little Red Riding Hood! Oh, what was she going to do?

Then, suddenly the cottage door flew open. There stood a very large and very strong woodsman! He was there to save Little Red Riding Hood!

Oh, the woodsman was very brave. And because he was so big and strong, he quickly convinced the wolf to leave.

Warren gave a nervous, but polite smile. Then with a giant leap, he jumped through the open window and out into the woods. He was never seen again.

Little Red Riding Hood was so relieved. She thanked the woodsman over and over again.

Just then there came more pounding on the closet door.

Little Red Riding Hood ran to the door and unlocked it. Out stepped her grandmother! They hugged again and again. The woodsman stood by, smiling.

Then Little Red Riding Hood, her grandmother and the woodsman sat down and feasted on the remaining blueberry muffins, and the peach preserves, and the herb tea. And when they finished, Little Red Riding Hood went straight home. She had learned that her mother was right. After that day, she always listened to her mother's advice, and she never left the path again!

 nd they all lived
happily ever after.